Autumn Whispers

Autumn Whispers

SECRETS IN THE FALLING LEAFS "LOVE IS A MYSTERY"

CORY WILSON

Contents

Introduction

THE AUTUMN LIFE

Samantha is an accomplished photographer and the proud owner of a charming bookstore nestled in a quaint town. As the vibrant colors of fall begin to paint the landscape, Samantha finds herself yearning for something more in her life. Despite her success, her heart remains untouched by the tender warmth of love. One crisp autumn day, she discovers a beautifully wrapped gift and a note at the doorstep of her bookstore. The note simply reads, "For the one who sees the world through a lens of beauty," and is accompanied by a bouquet of her favorite flowers. Intrigued, Samantha follows the clue to a picturesque park, where a man is waiting for her. He introduces himself as Ethan, a reserved yet kind-hearted man who has admired her from afar. Their connection is instant, but Ethan takes his time, allowing their love to blossom slowly. They share evenings in the glow of the setting sun, strolling through the golden-hued forests, exchanging slow kisses that linger like the crisp air of fall. Each encounter leaves Samantha yearning for more, as Ethan surprises her with thoughtful gifts and secret locations, always revealed through delicate notes and flowers. As they grow closer,

Samantha finds herself letting go of her guarded nature, opening up to the possibility of a deep, intimate love. Their relationship unfolds in the warmth of cozy bookstores, under the golden canopy of autumn leaves, and in the quiet moments of cuddling by the fire, where they share their dreams and secrets. But as Samantha's feelings deepen, she uncovers a secret from Ethan's past that threatens to disrupt the serenity they have built. Together, they must navigate the challenges of trust and forgiveness, learning that love, like the changing seasons, requires patience and a willingness to embrace the unknown. In the end, Samantha and Ethan's love story becomes a reflection of the season—full of gentle whispers, golden moments, and the promise of a new beginning as they prepare to face the winter together, stronger and more in love than ever before.

CHAPTER 1

The First Note

T he autumn air carried a crispness that hinted at the coming chill of winter, yet it was warm enough to enjoy the day without bundling up too tightly. The trees that lined the streets of the small town were ablaze with color—reds, oranges, and yellows that seemed to dance with every gentle breeze. Samantha Marshall pulled her coat a little tighter around her as she stepped out of her gold 2024 Nissan Rogue, admiring the way the fallen leaves crunched beneath her boots. Her bookstore, "Whispers in the Wind," was just as she had left it the night before—its windows adorned with garlands of autumn leaves and its sign swinging softly in the breeze. The shop was a sanctuary for many, a place where people could lose themselves in stories, just as she had count-less times. The scent of fresh coffee from the café next door mingled with the earthy aroma of old books, creating a warm and welcoming atmosphere that made Samantha smile every morning. As she approached the entrance, something caught her eye—a small, neatly wrapped package resting against the door. Her brow furrowed in curiosity. There was no name, no indication of who had left it, just a simple, elegant wrapping in

3

muted tones of gold and cream. A single white rose, her favorite, was tied to the top with a silk ribbon. Samantha glanced around, half-expecting to see someone watching her, but the street was quiet. She crouched down, carefully lifting the package and turning it over in her hands. It was light, and as she removed the ribbon and the flower, a note fluttered out, carried by the wind. She quickly caught it, her heart beginning to race. The note was written in elegant, flowing script on thick, cream-colored paper. It read: "For the one who sees the world through a lens of beauty." "Follow the path where the leaves fall gently, and you will find me waiting." A smile tugged at the corners of her lips as she read the words. There was something undeniably romantic about the gesture, something that stirred a long-forgotten part of her heart. She hadn't been involved with anyone in years, choosing instead to focus on her career and her bookstore. But this... this felt different. Curiosity piqued, Samantha tucked the note into her coat pocket and carefully unwrapped the package. Inside was a small, vintage-looking camera, its polished surface gleaming in the morning light. She turned it over in her hands, admiring the craftsmanship. It was the kind of camera that held stories of its own, capturing moments in a way that modern technology couldn't replicate. A sense of anticipation bubbled up inside her as she glanced around once more. There was no sign of who had left the gift, but the note's instructions were clear. Samantha locked the bookstore's door behind her and, with the camera in hand, began to walk down the path of fallen leaves that led away from the town center. The leaves crunched underfoot as she followed the trail, the vibrant colors creating a soft carpet that guided her steps. The town's streets were familiar, yet today, they felt different, as if the air itself were charged with possibility. The sun filtered through the trees, casting dappled shadows on the ground, and Samantha found herself slowing down, savoring the moment. The path led her to the town's park, a place she had often visited to clear her mind. It was a peaceful spot, with a small pond at its center and benches scattered around, offering a place to sit and reflect. Today, though, it felt like a destination, a place she was meant to be. As she entered the park, Samantha's eyes scanned the area, searching for the mysterious person who had left her the note and the gift. Her heart beat faster when she saw him —a man standing near the pond, his hands tucked into the pockets of a well-worn leather jacket. He was watching the water, seemingly lost in thought, but as if sensing her presence, he turned to face her. Their eyes met, and for a moment, the world seemed to be still. He had a calm, quiet presence about him, his gaze steady and warm. There was something familiar in his face, though Samantha couldn't place it. He smiled, and it was as though the autumn sun had come out from behind the clouds. "Hello, Samantha," he said, his voice smooth and rich, like the first sip of a well-brewed coffee. She stopped a few feet away from him, the camera still in her hands. "How do you know my name?" He chuckled softly, the sound low and comforting. "I've seen you around town, at your bookstore, and with your camera." "You have a way of capturing the world that's... captivating." Her heart fluttered at his words, but she kept her composure. "And the camera? The note?" "Consider it a gift," he replied, his eyes holding hers. "A way to start a journey that might lead to something beautiful." Samantha smiled, her curiosity turning into something deeper —an eagerness to learn more about this man who seemed to know her so well. "And what should I call you?" "Ethan," he answered, extending a hand. "Ethan Callahan." She took his hand, finding it warm and strong, a reassuring touch in the cool autumn air. "Nice to meet you, Ethan." "The pleasure is mine," he said, releasing her hand gently. "I hope you'll accept my invitation to continue this journey. There's much more to see, and I'd like to show it to you." Samantha looked around at the vibrant colors of fall, feeling the pull of something new and exciting. "I think I'd like that," she replied softly, her heart whispering the promise of what was to come.

CHAPTER 2

An Invitation

Ethan smiled at her response, a glint of something warm and sincere in his eyes that made Samantha feel like she had made the right choice. There was a quiet confidence about him, not overbearing but assured—like he knew exactly where they were going, even if she didn't yet. He gestured toward a nearby bench, one that offered a perfect view of the pond, its surface shimmering under the morning light. "Shall we sit for a while?" "The view is beautiful here, and it might give you some inspiration." Samantha nodded, following him to the bench. She was usually the one with the plan, the one who dictated the pace, but there was something comforting about letting Ethan take the lead. They sat side by side, close enough for her to feel the warmth of his presence but with just enough space to keep things innocent and respectful. The leaves continued to fall around them, a gentle reminder of the season's slow but inevitable change. Ethan leaned back, his gaze drifting over the pond. "I used to come here a lot as a kid. My grandparents lived in this town, and they'd bring me here whenever I visited. Back then, it felt like the whole world was in this little park." His voice had a nostalgic tone, one that resonated with Samantha. She knew that feeling—how certain places could hold the weight of memories, carrying them forward into the present. "It's a peaceful spot," she said, her own eyes tracing the ripples on the water. "I come here sometimes, too, especially when I need to think or clear my head." Ethan turned his gaze to her, studying her with quiet intensity. "I figured you might." "You have that look about you—like someone who sees more than just the surface of things." Samantha felt her cheeks warm under his scrutiny, but she didn't shy away. There was something disarming about Ethan, something that made her want to open up, even though they had only just met. "Photography helps with that," she said, turning the vintage camera over in her hands. "It forces you to focus on the details, to really see what's in front of you." "Sometimes, I think it's the only way I can make sense of the world." Ethan nodded as if he understood exactly what she meant. "That's why I thought you might like the camera. It's old, but it has a way of capturing moments that modern cameras can't. It makes you slow down and appreciate what's around you." Samantha smiled, touched by the thoughtfulness of his gift. "It's perfect," she said softly. "Thank you." He waved her thanks away with a modest shrug. "I'm glad you like it. There's something special about photography, especially in a place like this. The way the light plays off the water, the colors of the petals—it's all so fleeting. I thought you might want to capture it." There was a pause, the kind that didn't feel awkward but rather natural, as if they were both content just being in each other's presence. Samantha found herself relaxing, the usual tension she carried with her melting away in the quiet of the park. After a few moments, Ethan spoke again, his tone more serious. "I hope you don't mind me being a little forward, but there's something about you that I've been drawn to for a while now. I see you around town, always so focused, so passionate about what you do. It's rare to find someone who's so completely in tune with their world." Samantha was surprised by his honesty, but it wasn't unwelcome. There was a sincerity in his words that made her feel...seen, in a way she hadn't felt in a long time. "It's been a while since anyone's noticed that about me," she admitted, her voice quiet. "I've been so wrapped up in work, in running the bookstore, that I sometimes forget to look up and see the world for what it is." "That's understandable," Ethan said, leaning forward slightly, his eyes never leaving hers. "But it's also why I wanted to meet you." I think there's more to life than just what we do every day. Sometimes, we need someone to remind us of that, to show us that there's beauty in the simple things, in the moments we might otherwise overlook. His words resonated deeply with Samantha, stirring something inside her that she hadn't realized was missing. "You're right," she said, her voice a little stronger now. "I think I've been missing out on those moments." Ethan's smile was gentle and reassuring. "Then let's not miss out on them anymore. I'd like to show you something if you're up for it." Samantha hesitated for only a moment before nodding. "I'm up for it." He stood, offering her his hand. "There's a place nearby that I think you'll like. It's not far, and it's even more beautiful in the fall." Samantha took his hand, the warmth of his touch sending a pleasant shiver up her spine. She allowed him to lead her away from the park, through a narrow path that wound through the trees, their leaves rustling softly in the breeze. As they walked, Samantha couldn't help but feel that she was stepping into something new, something exciting and unknown. The path was narrow, and at times, they had to walk close together, their hands brushing occasionally, sending sparks of electricity between them. The further they walked, the more the town seemed to fade away, replaced by the quiet solitude of nature. After a short walk, they arrived at a small clearing. In the center stood a large oak tree, its branches heavy with golden leaves that swayed gently in the breeze. The ground beneath the tree was blanketed with fallen leaves, creating a soft, golden carpet. Ethan stopped and turned to her, his expression calm yet full of anticipation. "This is it," he said, his voice barely above a whisper. "I used to come here as a kid. It was my secret spot, where I'd come to think, to be alone with my thoughts. I haven't shared it with anyone in a long time, but I wanted to show it to you." Samantha looked around, taking in the beauty of the place. There was something magical about the clearing, something that made her feel as though they were the only two people in the world. The air was thick with the scent of earth and leafage, and the silence was broken only by the occasional rustle of the trees. "It's beautiful," she said, her voice soft and full of awe. "Thank you for bringing me here." Ethan smiled, a hint of relief in his eyes. "I'm glad you like it. I thought it might be a good place to get to know each other better." Samantha felt her heart flutter at his words. There was something about Ethan, something that made her want to know more, to understand the person behind the calm exterior. "I'd like that," she said, her voice steady despite the nervous excitement bubbling up inside her. They spent the next few hours in the clearing, talking about everything and nothing at all. Ethan shared stories from his childhood, tales of adventure and mischief that made Samantha laugh. In return, she told him about her life, her love for photography, and the challenges of running a bookstore in a small town. As the afternoon sun began to dip lower in the sky, casting long shadows across the clearing, Samantha felt a sense of peace that she hadn't felt in years. Being with Ethan was easy, natural, like they'd known each other far longer than a few hours. Eventually, they fell into a comfortable silence, sitting side by side on the soft bed of fronds. The sun dipped below the horizon, casting the clearing in a warm, golden glow. Samantha felt Ethan's arm brush against hers, a small, almost accidental touch that sent a wave of warmth through her. She turned to him, finding him watching her with that same quiet intensity. There was something unspoken in the air between them, something that made her heart race and her breath catch in her throat. She realized that she wanted him to kiss her, to close the small distance between them and make this moment something more. But Ethan didn't move, didn't push for anything more. Instead, he simply smiled, his eyes full of understanding. "I'm glad we met today," he said softly, his voice full of sincerity. "Me too," Samantha whispered, her heart pounding in her chest. She wanted to lean in, to close the gap between them, but something held her back—a desire to savor this moment, to let it unfold naturally. Ethan seemed to sense her hesitation, and he didn't press. Instead, he reached out and gently took her hand in his, his thumb brushing softly against her skin. "I'd like to see you again, Samantha," he said, his voice low and full of promise. Samantha felt a smile tug at the corners of her lips. "I'd like that too," she replied, her voice barely above a whisper. They sat there for a while longer, holding hands as the day slowly turned into evening, the golden light giving way to the soft, dusky hues of twilight. It was a moment suspended in time, a perfect beginning to something that neither of them could fully predict, but both were eager to explore. As they walked back to town together, their hands still intertwined, Samantha couldn't help but feel that this was the start of something beautiful—something that would change her life in ways she couldn't yet imagine. And as they parted ways at the edge of the park, with Ethan promising to leave another note soon, she knew that she would be waiting eagerly for whatever came next.

CHAPTER 3

The Second Note

The next morning, Samantha awoke with a sense of anticipation, a feeling that something wonderful was just around the corner. The memory of her time with Ethan filled her mind as she got ready for the day. His gentle smile, the warmth of his hand in hers, and the way he seemed to understand her in a way that few people ever had—it all played on a loop in her thoughts. After a quick breakfast, Samantha headed to her bookstore. The shop was a cozy haven, nestled between two larger buildings on the main street of the small town. Its wooden sign, weathered with age, read "Whispering Pages," and inside, the scent of old books blended with the faint aroma of coffee from the small café in the corner. As Samantha unlocked the door and stepped inside, she couldn't help but glance around, half-expecting to see another note from Ethan. She smiled at the thought, already looking forward to whatever surprise he had planned next. The day passed in a blur of activity. Customers came and went, browsing the shelves, chatting with Samantha about their latest reads, and sipping coffee in the café. Despite the busyness, Samantha's mind kept drifting back to Ethan, wondering when she might see him again. It was late afternoon when she finally found the note. She was organizing a display near the front of the store when something caught her eye—a small envelope, tucked neatly between two books on the shelf. Her heart skipped a beat as she pulled it out, recognizing Ethan's neat handwriting on the front: "Samantha." With a quick glance around to make sure no one was watching, Samantha opened the envelope and pulled out the note inside. "Dear Samantha," it began, "I hope this note finds you well." "I enjoyed our time together yesterday more than I can say." "There's something about you that draws me in, like a story that I can't wait to keep reading." If you're free this evening, I'd love to take you to another one of my favorite spots. Meet me at the edge of the forest, where the old oak tree stands, just as the sun begins to set. I'll be waiting. Samantha's heart fluttered as she read the note. There was something undeniably romantic about the way Ethan left these messages, the way he seemed to know just how to pique her curiosity and draw her in. She felt a thrill of excitement at the thought of seeing him again, of discovering what he had planned next. She carefully folded the note and slipped it into her pocket, a small smile playing on her lips. The rest of the day passed in a haze of anticipation, her thoughts consumed by the promise of another evening with Ethan. As the sun began to dip lower in the sky, casting long shadows across the town, Samantha closed up the bookstore and headed home to freshen up. She chose a simple but elegant outfit—a soft sweater in a warm autumnal shade, paired with dark jeans and her favorite boots. It was comfortable but stylish, the kind of outfit that made her feel confident and at ease. With one last glance in the mirror, Samantha grabbed her jacket and headed out the door. The air was cool, with just a hint of the coming evening's chill, and the leaves crunched underfoot as she made her way to the meeting spot. The forest was just on the edge of town, a place where the trees grew tall and thick, their branches intertwining to form a natural canopy. The old oak tree that Ethan had mentioned was easy to spot—its gnarled trunk and sprawling branches made it stand out among the others. As Samantha approached the tree, she saw him standing there, waiting for her. He was dressed casually, in a dark jacket and jeans, but there was something about the way he stood, the way he looked at her as she approached, that made her heart skip a beat. "Right on time," Ethan said, his voice warm and welcoming as she reached him. Samantha smiled, feeling a little breathless as she stood before him. "I wouldn't miss it for the world," she replied, her voice soft. He reached out and took her hand, his touch sending a familiar warmth through her. "Come on," he said, leading her toward a narrow path that wound its way deeper into the forest. "There's something I want to show you." They walked together, side by side, their hands clasped as they made their way along the path. The forest was quiet, save for the occasional rustle of leaves and the soft calls of birds settling in for the night. The air was cool, but with Ethan by her side, Samantha felt nothing but warmth. As they walked, the trees gradually began to thin, and soon they emerged into a small clearing. In the center of the clearing was a small, tranquil pond, its surface perfectly still, reflecting the deepening colors of the evening sky. Around the pond, the ground was carpeted with fallen leaves, their rich hues of red, orange, and gold glowing in the fading light. Ethan led her to a spot near the water's edge, where a blanket had been spread out on the ground. A small picnic basket sat nearby, and a couple of lanterns provided a soft, flickering light that added to the enchanting atmosphere. "I thought we could have a little picnic," Ethan said, his voice gentle as he guided her to sit beside him on the blanket. "I hope you don't mind." Samantha was touched by the thoughtfulness of it all. "This is perfect," she said, her voice full of warmth. "Thank you." They sat together, sharing the simple meal Ethan had prepared—fresh bread, cheese, fruit, and a bottle of wine. The conversation flowed easily, as it had the day before, with each of them sharing stories and laughing together. The more time Samantha spent with Ethan, the more she felt drawn to him, as if a connection were forming between them that went beyond mere attraction. As the last rays of sunlight dipped below the horizon, leaving the clearing bathed in the soft glow of the lanterns, the conversation grew quieter, more intimate. Samantha found herself leaning closer to Ethan, her heart racing as their hands brushed and their shoulders touched. At one point, Ethan turned to her, his gaze intense and searching. "Samantha," he began, his voice low, "there's something I've been wanting to tell you." Her heart skipped a beat, the air between them thick with anticipation. "What is it?" she asked, her voice barely above a whisper. Ethan reached up, gently brushing a stray strand of hair from her face, his touch light and tender. "I know we've only just met, but I feel like there's something special between us," he said, his eyes never leaving hers. "Something I don't want to ignore." Samantha's breath caught in her throat, her heart pounding as his words sank in. "I feel it too," she admitted, her voice trembling slightly with emotion. "I've never felt this way before, not so quickly." Ethan smiled, a look of relief and happiness washing over his face. "I'm glad," he said softly. "Because I want to take things slow, to really get to know you, but I also don't want to waste a single moment." Samantha's heart swelled with emotion, a mixture of joy and nervous excitement. She could feel the same desire within herself—to take their time, to savor every moment, but also to embrace whatever was growing between them. Without thinking, she leaned in closer, her eyes drifting to his lips. Ethan seemed to understand, and he closed the distance between them, his hand gently cradling her cheek as he pressed his lips to hers in a soft, lingering kiss. It was a kiss full of promise, of unspoken feelings, and as they pulled away, Samantha felt a warmth spread through her entire being. They sat there for a while longer, their hands interlaced, the kiss lingering in the air between them. The night had fully settled in by the time they decided to leave the clearing, the lanterns casting long shadows as they packed up the picnic. Ethan walked her back to the edge of the forest, their hands still clasped, and when they reached her car, he paused, turning to face her. "Thank you for tonight," Samantha said, her voice full of sincerity. "It was perfect." Ethan smiled, his eyes soft and warm in the dim light. "I'm glad you enjoyed it," he said. "I'll be thinking of you until I see you again." Samantha felt a thrill of excitement at his words, already looking forward to their next meeting. "I will too," she replied, her voice soft. He leaned in and kissed her again, a brief but tender kiss that left her feeling breathless. "Goodnight, Samantha," he said as he pulled away, his hand lingering in hers for a moment longer. "Goodnight, Ethan," she whispered, watching as he turned and walked away, his figure soon swallowed by the darkness of the forest. As she drove home, her heart was light, her thoughts filled with the promise of what was to come. The night had been everything she could have hoped for—romantic, intimate, and full of the kind of quiet magic that she'd always dreamed of finding. And as she lay in bed that night, the memory of Ethan's kiss still tingling on her lips, Samantha knew that this was only the beginning of something truly special.

CHAPTER 4

Autumn's Embrace

The days that followed were filled with an intoxicating blend of anticipation and contentment. Samantha found herself replaying the moments with Ethan over and over in her mind—his gentle touch, the way he looked at her, the warmth of his presence. It was a feeling she hadn't experienced before, and it left her both excited and a little scared. Ethan's notes continued to arrive, each one as thoughtful and romantic as the last. Sometimes, he would leave them at her bookstore, tucked between the pages of her favorite novels or hidden among the autumn leaves near her car. Other times, she would find a note on her doorstep, accompanied by a bouquet of her favorite flowers—lilies, their sweet fragrance filling her home with memories of him. The messages were always simple, yet filled with affection: "Thinking of you," "I can't wait to see you again," or "Meet me by the lake tonight at dusk." Each note brought a flutter to her heart, a sense of connection that grew stronger with every passing day. One crisp autumn afternoon, as the leaves swirled in the breeze and the golden light of the setting sun bathed the town in a warm glow, Samantha received another note. This one was different, though—slightly longer and more personal. "Dear Samantha," it began. "I've been thinking a lot about us lately. I know we've been taking things slow, and I want you to know that I'm so grateful for every moment we've shared. But there's something I need to tell you, something I've been holding back." Samantha's heart raced as she read the words, her fingers trembling slightly as she turned the page. "There's a part of me that's afraid of what might happen if I let myself fall for you completely," the note continued. But there's also a part of me that knows that if I don't take that leap, I might miss out on something truly wonderful. So tonight, I want to take that step. "Meet me at the old stone bridge at midnight. I have something important to say." Her breath caught in her throat as she finished reading, the note slipping from her fingers and fluttering to the floor. Midnight at the old stone bridge—it was a place she had always found beautiful but slightly eerie, especially in the quiescence of the night. The thought of meeting Ethan there, under the cover of darkness, filled her with a mixture of excitement and nervousness. That evening, Samantha could hardly focus on anything else. She closed the bookstore early, her mind too preoccupied to concentrate on work. She spent hours at home, pacing the floor and trying to steady her nerves. She wanted to believe that this was the beginning of something even deeper, but there was a part of her that feared what Ethan might have to say. As the clock neared midnight, Samantha found herself standing in front of the mirror, smoothing down the soft fabric of her dress—a deep burgundy color that matched the autumn leaves outside. She wrapped a scarf around her neck and slipped on a pair of boots, her hands trembling slightly as she pulled on her coat. The drive to the old stone bridge was a short one, but it felt like an eternity. The town was quiet at this hour, the streets deserted, and the only sound was the soft hum of her car's engine. The moon hung low in the sky, casting a silvery light over the landscape, and the air was cool and crisp, filled with the scent of earth and fallen leaves. When she arrived at the bridge, Samantha parked her car a short distance away and walked the rest of the way, the gravel crunching underfoot as she approached. The bridge was a small, arching structure made of weathered stone that had stood the test of time. It spanned a narrow creek, the water below murmuring softly as it flowed beneath. Ethan was already there, leaning against the stone railing, his silhouette outlined against the moonlit sky. He turned as she approached, his eyes meeting hers with an intensity that made her breath catch. "Samantha," he said softly as she reached him, his voice carrying over the stillness of the night. "Ethan," she replied, her voice barely above a whisper. For a moment, they stood there in silence, and the only sounds were the rustle of leaves in the breeze and the gentle flow of the creek below. Then Ethan stepped closer, reaching out to take her hands in his. His touch was warm, steadying her as she looked up at him, her heart racing. "I'm glad you came," he said, his voice low and filled with emotion. "I couldn't stay away," she admitted, her eyes searching his face for some sign of what was to come. Ethan hesitated for a moment, as if gathering his thoughts, then took a deep breath. "Samantha, I've been holding back because... I've been hurt before." "I've had people walk out on me when I thought things were going well, and it's made me cautious, afraid to let myself fall too quickly." Samantha's heart ached at his words, the vulnerability in his voice tugging at her emotions. "I understand," she said softly, squeezing his hands. "I've been hurt too. But I don't want to let that fear stop me from finding something real." Ethan nodded, his eyes softening as he gazed at her. "I feel the same way. And I don't want to hold back anymore. I want to be with you, Samantha. I want to see where this can go, without any reservations." A wave of relief and happiness washed over her, and she felt tears puncture at the corners of her eyes. "I want that too," she whispered, her voice thick with emotion. Without another word, Ethan pulled her into his arms, holding her close as if he never wanted to let go. Samantha buried her face in his chest, breathing in his scent and feeling the steady beat of his heart against her own. It was a moment of pure connection, of shared understanding, and it filled her with a sense of peace she hadn't known she was missing. They stayed like that for a long time, wrapped in each other's arms, the world around them forgotten. The night was cold, but with Ethan's arms around her, Samantha felt nothing but warmth. Eventually, Ethan pulled back just enough to tilt her chin up, his gaze locking with hers. "Samantha," he said softly, "I think I'm falling in love with you." Her breath caught at his words, and for a moment, she could only stare at him, her heart pounding in her chest. Then, slowly, she smiled—a soft, radiant smile that lit up her entire face. "I think I'm falling in love with you too, Ethan," she whispered. A look of pure happiness crossed his face, and he leaned in, capturing her lips in a kiss that was gentle, tender, and filled with all the emotions they had just avowed. The kiss deepened slowly, a dance of lips and breath that left them both breathless and longing for more. When they finally pulled apart, Ethan rested his forehead against hers, his breath mingling with hers in the cool night air. "I don't want this night to end," he murmured, his voice low and full of emotion. "Neither do I," Samantha whispered back, her heart swelling with a mixture of joy and contentment. They spent the rest of the night on the bridge, talking, laughing, and sharing quiet moments as the stars wheeled overhead and the world around them slept. By the time the first light of dawn began to color the horizon, they knew they had found something truly special—something worth holding on to, no matter what the future might bring. As they walked back to Samantha's car, hand in hand, the leaves rustling underfoot, she couldn't help but feel that this was just the beginning of their story. The beginning of an autumn that would linger in her heart forever, a season of love and warmth that would carry them through whatever lay ahead.

CHAPTER 5

First Brightness of Love

The next few weeks passed in a beautiful blur for Samantha. She and Ethan spent nearly every day together, their bond growing deeper with each moment they shared. The autumn air grew cooler, and the leaves continued to fall in a cascade of gold, red, and brown, creating a picturesque backdrop for their blossoming love. One evening, after a long day at the bookstore, Samantha received another note from Ethan. This time, it was slipped into the pocket of her coat while she wasn't looking. The simple elegance of his gesture brought a smile to her face. "Meet me at the orchard just before sunset. I have a surprise for you." Samantha's heart skipped a beat. The orchard had always been one of her favorite places—a serene haven just outside of town, where the trees stood tall and proud, their branches heavy with ripe apples in the autumn season. She had taken countless photographs there, capturing the beauty of nature in all its quiet splendor. Excited for whatever Ethan had planned, Samantha hurried home to freshen up. She chose a cozy, cream-colored sweater that complemented her soft brown eyes and paired it with her favorite pair of jeans. After brushing her hair until it shone like silk, she slipped on her boots and headed out the door. The drive to the orchard was peaceful, the road winding through the countryside, flanked by rows of trees shedding their leaves. The sky was a canvas of warm hues—pinks, oranges, and purples blending together as the sun began its descent. Samantha arrived at the orchard just as the last rays of sunlight filtered through the trees, casting long shadows on the ground. As she stepped out of her car, she saw Ethan waiting for her near the entrance to the orchard, leaning casually against a wooden fence. He smiled as she approached, his eyes lighting up as they always did when he saw her. "You made it," he said, stepping forward to greet her with a gentle kiss on the cheek. The touch of his lips sent a shiver down her spine, a reminder of the connection they shared. "Of course," Samantha replied, smiling up at him. "I wouldn't miss it for anything. So, what's this surprise you mentioned?" Ethan grinned, a mischievous glint in his eyes. "You'll see. But first, we have to take a little walk." He took her hand, and they began to stroll through the orchard. The trees were ablaze with color, their leaves crunching beneath their feet as they walked. The air was filled with the sweet scent of apples, mingling with the crispness of the fall breeze. It was the kind of evening that made Samantha feel alive, her senses heightened by the beauty around her and the warmth of Ethan's hand in hers. As they walked, Ethan talked about his day, sharing little stories that made her laugh. He had a way of making even the most mundane things sound interesting, and she loved listening to him. In return, she told him about the customers at her bookstore, the quirky regulars who came in just to chat, and the new photography project she was working on. Eventually, they reached a clearing in the orchard, where the trees opened up to reveal a breathtaking view of the horizon. The sun was just a sliver of reveal on the edge of the sky, casting a golden glow over everything. Samantha gasped in surprise when she saw what Ethan had done. In the middle of the clearing, he had set up a picnic blanket, surrounded by lanterns that flickered softly in the evening light. A basket sat in the center of the blanket, and beside it, a bouquet of her favorite lilies. "Ethan, this is... incredible," she whispered, her voice filled with awe. "You did all this for me?" Ethan nodded, his smile tender as he watched her reaction. "I wanted to do something special for you." "You've brought so much light into my life, Samantha. I wanted to give you a little piece of that light back." Tears of happiness welled up in Samantha's eyes as she stepped forward, wrapping her arms around Ethan and holding him close. "You're amazing," she whispered into his chest, feeling his arms encircle her in return. "Thank you." They sat down together on the blanket, the warmth of the lanterns surrounding them as they shared the picnic Ethan had prepared. He had brought her favorite foods—cheese and crackers, fresh bread, slices of apple pie, and a bottle of crisp white wine. As they ate, they talked about their dreams, their hopes for the future, and the things that made them who they were. The conversation flowed effortlessly, the connection between them growing stronger with every word, every laugh, and every shared glance. As the night wore on, the stars began to appear in the sky, twinkling like diamonds against the deep blue canvas above. After they finished eating, Ethan leaned back on the blanket, pulling Samantha with him so they could gaze up at the stars together. She nestled against him, her head resting on his shoulder, and he wrapped an arm around her, holding her close. "This is perfect," Samantha murmured, her voice soft as she stared up at the sky. "I can't imagine being anywhere else. "I feel the same way," Ethan replied, his voice a low rumble in the stillness of the night. "Being with you... it's like everything just falls into place." They lay there in comfortable silence for a while, the world around them quiet except for the occasional rustle of leaves in the breeze. Samantha felt a sense of contentment settle over her, a feeling of peace that she hadn't known in a long time. After a while, Ethan shifted slightly, turning to look at her. "Samantha," he began, his tone serious, "there's something I need to tell you." She turned her head to meet his gaze, her heart skipping a beat at the intensity in his eyes. "What is it?" she asked, her voice barely above a whisper. Ethan hesitated for a moment, as if choosing his words carefully. "I've been thinking a lot about us," he said slowly. "And... I want you to know that I'm ready. I'm ready to let go of my fears, to stop holding back. I want to be with you completely. No reservations, no doubts." Samantha's breath caught in her throat, her heart swelling with emotion. She reached out, cupping his face in her hand, her thumb brushing lightly over his cheek. "Ethan, I... I feel the same way." I want that too. A look of relief and happiness crossed his face, and he leaned in, capturing her lips in a kiss that was slow and deep, filled with all the emotions they had been holding back. Samantha melted into the kiss, her arms wrapping around him as she let herself get lost in the moment. When they finally pulled apart, Ethan rested his forehead against hers, his breath warm against her skin. "I love you, Samantha," he whispered, the words like a promise, a vow. Tears of joy filled her eyes as she smiled, her heart so full she thought it might burst. "I love you too, Ethan," she whispered back, her voice thick with emotion. They kissed again, a slow, lingering kiss that seemed to seal the bond between them, solidifying the love that had been growing ever since that first fateful encounter. As they held each other under the blanket of stars, surrounded by the beauty of the autumn night, Samantha knew that this was just the beginning of their story. The beginning of an endless season of love and warmth, where they would face the future together, hand in hand, no matter what came their way.

CHAPTER 6

A New Embrace

The days following that magical night in the orchard were a dream come true for Samantha. Each morning, she woke up with a smile on her face, knowing that Ethan would be a part of her day. Their relationship had deepened, and with it, an unspoken understanding that what they shared was real and lasting. One crisp autumn morning, Samantha was in her bookstore, organizing a new shipment of books. The scent of freshly printed pages filled the air, blending with the aroma of cinnamon and vanilla from the candles she had lit. The shop was quiet, the early hour keeping most customers at bay, giving her time to enjoy the peaceful solitude. As she placed a stack of novels on a shelf, the bell above the door jingled, signaling that someone had entered. She turned around, expecting to see one of her regulars, but her heart skipped a beat when she saw Ethan standing there, a warm smile on his face."Good morning," he greeted, his voice like a soothing melody. He was dressed casually in a navy sweater and jeans, his hair slightly tousled from the stylish wind outside."Good morning," Samantha replied, her smile mirroring his. "What brings you here so early?" "I wanted to see you," he said simply, as if that were the most natural thing in the world. He approached her, holding out a small bouquet of lilies—her favorite. "And I thought these might brighten your day." Samantha's heart swelled with affection as she took the flowers from him, inhaling their sweet fragrance. "You're too good to me, Ethan," she said softly, touched by his thoughtfulness. "I just want to make you happy," he replied, his eyes locking with hers. "You deserve nothing less." They stood there for a moment, the world around them fading away as they lost themselves in each other's gaze. Finally, Ethan broke the silence, clearing his throat as if to shake off the intensity of the moment. "So," he said, a playful smile tugging at the corners of his mouth, "do you have any plans for tonight?"Samantha raised an eyebrow, intrigued by his tone. "Not yet. Why do you ask?" "Well," Ethan began, taking a step closer to her, "I was thinking... maybe we could spend the evening together. I have something special planned."Samantha's curiosity piqued. "Special, huh? Should I be worried?" He chuckled, shaking his head. "No, definitely not. Just be ready by six, and I'll pick you up. It's a bit of a surprise." Her excitement bubbled up at the thought of another one of Ethan's surprises. "I can't wait," she said, her eyes sparkling with anticipation. True to his word, Ethan arrived at her place promptly at six. Samantha had spent the afternoon getting ready, choosing a soft, burgundy sweater dress that accentuated her figure and paired it with black ankle boots. She kept her makeup light, just enough to highlight her natural beauty and let her hair fall in loose waves around her shoulders. When she opened the door, Ethan's eyes lit up with admiration. "You look stunning," he said, leaning in to kiss her softly on the lips. "Thank you," she replied, her cheeks flushing slightly. "You're not so bad yourself." Ethan had dressed up for the occasion, wearing a crisp white shirt under a tailored black coat, his dark jeans and polished shoes completing the look. He offered her his arm, and together, they walked to his car, the evening air cool and refreshing. As they drove through the town, the streets lined with trees shedding their autumn leaves, Samantha couldn't help but feel a sense of contentment. The last few weeks had been a whirlwind, but every moment with Ethan had felt right, like they were exactly where they were meant to be. After a short drive, Ethan pulled into a small, secluded parking lot at the edge of town. Samantha recognized the area—it was near the lake, a quiet spot that was often overlooked by most of the townspeople."Where are we going?" she asked, her curiosity growing. Ethan smiled mysteriously. "You'll see."They got out of the car, and Ethan led her down a narrow path that wound through a grove of trees. The sound of leaves crunching underfoot filled the air, and the scent of pine and earth surrounded them. The sky was beginning to darken, the sun dipping below the horizon, casting long shadows on the ground.Finally, they emerged from the trees and found themselves at the edge of the lake. Samantha gasped in surprise. The area had been transformed into a magical setting. Lanterns hung from the branches of the surrounding trees, their soft light reflecting off the calm surface of the water. A blanket was spread out on the ground, with pillows and a basket sitting atop it. Nearby, a small fire pit crackled softly, adding warmth to the chilly evening."This is beautiful," Samantha whispered, her eyes wide with wonder.Ethan took her hand, leading her to the blanket. "I wanted to create a special moment for us," he said softly. "A place where we can just be... together." They sat down on the blanket, the fire casting a warm glow over them. Ethan reached into the basket and pulled out a bottle of wine, pouring them each a glass. As they sipped their drinks, the conversation flowed naturally, each word drawing them closer together.After a while, Ethan set his glass aside and reached for Samantha's hand, his touch gentle and comforting. "There's something I've been wanting to tell you," he said, his voice low and earnest. Samantha's heart fluttered, a mixture of anticipation and nerves. "What is it?" she asked, her eyes searching his. Ethan took a deep breath, as if gathering his thoughts. "Samantha, these past few weeks have been incredible. I've never met anyone like you—someone who makes me feel so alive, so understood. I've fallen for you, completely and utterly. And I want to be with you, not just for now, but for the long haul." Tears welled up in Samantha's eyes as she listened to his words, her heart swelling with love for the man sitting in front of her. She had known, deep down, that this was where their journey was heading, but hearing him say it out loud made it all the more real. "I feel the same way, Ethan," she whispered, her voice trembling with emotion. "I've fallen for you too, and I can't imagine my life without you in it." A look of pure happiness spread across Ethan's face, and he leaned in, capturing her lips in a kiss that was both affectionate and passionate. Samantha responded eagerly, her arms wrapping around his neck as she melted into him. The kiss deepened, their connection growing stronger with each passing second. They pulled each other closer, the rest of the world fading away as they focused on the warmth of their embrace, the sweetness of the moment.When they finally broke apart, they rested their foreheads together, their breaths mingling in the cool night air. "I love you, Samantha," Ethan whispered, his voice filled with sincerity."I love you too, Ethan," she replied, her heart soaring with happiness. They spent the rest of the evening wrapped in each other's arms, talking about their dreams for the future, their hopes and fears, and everything in between. The fire crackled softly beside them, the lanterns casting a soft glow over the scene, and the lake shimmered under the light of the rising moon. It was a night that marked the beginning of a new chapter in their lives—a chapter filled with love, trust, and the promise of a future together. As they held each other close, surrounded by the beauty of the autumn night, they knew that this was only the start of something truly special.

CHAPTER 7

Falling Leaves, Rising Love

In the days that followed, Samantha and Ethan's relationship flourished, their love growing stronger with each passing moment. The town was alive with the spirit of fall, the streets lined with pumpkins and scarecrows, the trees a riot of color as the leaves continued to fall. The crisp air carried the scent of wood smoke and spiced cider, and everywhere they went, there was a feeling of warmth and coziness. Samantha had never been happier. Her days were filled with the simple pleasures of life—morning coffee with Ethan, afternoons spent at the bookstore surrounded by the comforting smell of books, and evenings that ended with sweet kisses and whispered words of love. One afternoon, while Samantha was arranging a display of new arrivals at the bookstore, the door chimed, and she looked up to see Ethan walking in, a mischievous grin on his face. "Hey, you," she greeted him, her heart fluttering at the sight of him. "Hey," he replied, leaning across the counter to swipe a quick kiss. "I was thinking... how about we take a little road trip this weekend? Just the two of us." Samantha's eyes lit up with excitement. "That sounds amazing! Where do you want to go?" Ethan shrugged, his grin widening. "I was thinking we could just drive and see where the road takes us. Maybe head to the mountains, do some hiking, and take in the fall colors." Samantha loved the idea. There was something exhilarating about the thought of just getting in the car and driving, with no set destination, no plan —just them and the open road. "Let's do it," she agreed, feeling a surge of anticipation. "It sounds perfect." The weekend came quickly, and early on Saturday morning, they packed up the Nissan Rogue with blankets, snacks, and a camera for capturing the beautiful fall scenery. Samantha felt a thrill of excitement as they set off into the frosty morning air.

The weekend came quickly, and early on Saturday morning, they packed up the Nissan Rogue with blankets, snacks, and a camera for capturing the beautiful fall scenery. Samantha felt a thrill of excitement as they set off, the cool morning air crisp with the promise of adventure. As they drove out of town, the city slowly gave way to the open road, the landscape shifting from suburban streets to winding country roads lined with vibrant trees. The colors of autumn were at their peak—rich reds, oranges, and yellows blending together like a painting. Samantha rolled down the window, letting the fresh air fill the car, and sighed in contentment. Ethan reached over, taking her hand in his, and gave it a gentle squeeze. "This is nice, isn't it?" he said, his voice warm with affection. "It really is," Samantha agreed, glancing over at him with a smile. "I love spending time like this with you." "No distractions, just us and the road." They drove for a few hours, the conversation flowing easily between them, touching on everything from their favorite childhood memories to their dreams for the future. Every once in a while, Ethan would point out a particularly beautiful view, and they would pull over to take a picture or simply admire the scenery. As the day wore on, they found themselves in a quaint little mountain town nestled in the valley. The town was charming, with cobblestone streets and old-fashioned storefronts adorned with fall decorations. The scent of freshly baked pies and spiced cider wafted through the air, inviting them to explore. Ethan parked the car, and they spent the afternoon wandering through the town, hand in hand. They stopped at a cozy café for lunch, enjoying bowls of hearty soup and warm bread, then browsed the local shops, picking up a few small souvenirs to remember the trip by. In the late afternoon, as the sun began to dip lower in the sky, they found a trail that led up into the mountains. It was a quiet path, the only sounds were the rustling of leaves underfoot and the occasional chirping of birds. The air grew cooler as they climbed higher, and Samantha pulled her coat tighter around her, relishing the briskness. When they reached a clearing with a breathtaking view of the valley below, they decided to stop and rest. The sun was setting, shaping a golden glow over the landscape, and the sky was painted with streaks of pink and orange. Ethan spread out a blanket, and they sat down, taking in the view. Samantha leaned into him, resting her head on his shoulder, and he wrapped his arm around her, pulling her close. "This is perfect," Samantha murmured, her voice filled with contentment. "I don't think I've ever been this happy." Ethan turned his head slightly, pressing a soft kiss to her temple. "I'm glad," he said quietly. "Because I feel the same way." They sat there in comfortable silence for a while, simply enjoying the peacefulness of the moment. As the last rays of sunlight disappeared behind the mountains, the stars began to twinkle overhead, one by one. The sky was clear, and the night air was crisp, with just a hint of wood smoke from a distant fire. After a while, Ethan reached into his jacket pocket and pulled out a small, wrapped package. "I have something for you," he said, handing it to Samantha. Surprised, Samantha took the package and carefully unwrapped it. Inside was a delicate silver necklace with a small, intricate leaf pendant. The leaf was detailed, with tiny veins etched into the metal, and it shimmered in the fading light. "It's beautiful," Samantha breathed, touched by the thoughtful gift. She looked up at Ethan, her eyes shining. "Thank you." "It reminded me of you," Ethan said softly, his gaze locked on hers. "Elegant, timeless, and full of life." Samantha's heart swelled with emotion as she leaned in to kiss him, her lips brushing his in a gentle, lingering kiss. "I love it," she whispered against his lips. "And I love you." "I love you too," Ethan whispered back, his voice full of warmth and certainty. They stayed like that for a long time, holding each other close as the stars continued to shine above them, the night wrapping around them like a protective blanket. It was in moments like these that Samantha knew she had found something rare and precious—true love, the kind that would last a lifetime. As they eventually packed up and made their way back down the trail, their hands intertwined, Samantha couldn't help but feel that this trip had solidified their bond even further. They were not just two people in love; they were partners, best friends, and soulmates, ready to face whatever life had in store for them.

CHAPTER 8

Whispers of Forever

The next few weeks were a whirlwind of activity as Samantha and Ethan continued to build their life together. The town was fully immersed in the spirit of fall, with festivals, fairs, and events happening nearly every weekend. Samantha loved every minute of it, especially since she got to experience it all with Ethan by her side. One crisp Saturday morning, as they were enjoying breakfast at a quaint little café downtown, Ethan leaned across the table with a serious expression on his face. "I've been thinking," he began, his tone thoughtful. "About us. About the future." Samantha's heart skipped a beat. "What about it?" she asked, her voice steady despite the flutter of nerves in her stomach. Ethan reached for her hand, his touch reassuring. "I want to spend the rest of my life with you, Samantha." "I know it's only been a short time, but I've never been more sure of anything in my life." "You make me better." "You make me happy." Tears welled up in Samantha's eyes as she listened to his words, her heart swelling with love and gratitude. "I feel the same way, Ethan," she said softly. "I can't imagine my life without you in it." Ethan smiled, a look of relief and joy crossing his features.

"I want to take the next step," he continued, his voice filled with determination. "I want us to move in together, to start building our life together every day." Samantha was momentarily speechless; the idea of living with Ethan was both thrilling and a little overwhelming. But as she looked into his eyes, she knew that it was the right decision. They were meant to be together, and this was the natural next step. "I'd love that," she finally said, her voice filled with truthfulness. "I want to be with you every day." Ethan's smile widened, and he squeezed her hand. "Then let's do it. Let's find a place that's ours. A place where we can build our future." The rest of the day was spent driving around town, looking at potential homes, and discussing their dreams for the future. They talked about everything—from what kind of house they wanted to how they would decorate it, to the possibility of starting a family one day. As the sun began to set, they found themselves standing in front of a charming little cottage on the outskirts of town. The house was cozy and inviting, with a wraparound porch and a garden full of autumn flowers. The inside was just as perfect, with a fireplace, hardwood floors, and plenty of space for the two of them to grow. "I think this is it," Samantha said, her voice filled with awe as she took in the space. "It feels like home." Ethan nodded, his eyes filled with the same sense of certainty. "It does. This is where we're supposed to be." They made an offer on the house that evening, and within a few days, it was theirs. The next few weeks were a blur of packing, moving, and settling into their new home. But through it all, Samantha couldn't shake the feeling that she was exactly where she was meant to be—by Ethan's side, building a life full of love, laughter, and endless possibilities. As they unpacked the last of the boxes and sat together on the couch in front of the fireplace, Samantha leaned into Ethan, feeling the warmth of the fire and the comfort of his presence. "This is just the beginning," Ethan murmured, his arm wrapped around her shoulders. "We have so much to look forward to." Samantha smiled, closing her eyes and savoring the moment. "I know," she whispered. "And I can't wait to see what the future holds." As the flames sparked softly in the fireplace and the autumn leaves rustled outside, Samantha knew that this was more than just the start of a new chapter in their lives—it was the beginning of their forever.

Whispers of Forever
(Continued)

CHAPTER 8

The first few nights in their new home were magical. Samantha and Ethan spent their evenings curled up by the fireplace, sipping hot cocoa and talking about everything and nothing. The house was still full of unpacked boxes, but neither of them minded. They were too busy making new memories, filling the space with laughter and love. One evening, after a particularly busy day of arranging furniture and hanging pictures, Ethan surprised Samantha with a candlelit dinner. He'd picked up her favorite meal from the little Italian restaurant downtown and set the table with fresh flowers and soft music playing in the background. "Ethan, this is amazing," Samantha said as she walked into the dining room, her heart swelling with affection for him. "I thought we could use a little break," Ethan replied with a grin, pulling out a chair for her. "Besides, I wanted to do something special for you." "To celebrate us." They sat down together, the flickering candlelight casting a warm glow over the room. As they ate, they talked about their plans for the future—trips they wanted to take, projects they wanted to work on, and dreams they hoped to fulfill together. After dinner, Ethan took Samantha's hand and led her outside to the porch. The night was cool, with a gentle breeze rustling through the trees. The sky was clear, and the stars shone brightly overhead. "Close your eyes," Ethan whispered, his voice soft and full of anticipation. Samantha did as he asked, her heart fluttering with curiosity. She felt Ethan's hands gently guiding her, and then the sensation of something cool and metal slipping around her neck. "Okay, open them," Ethan said. Samantha opened her eyes and looked down to see the silver leaf pendant he'd given her weeks ago now hanging from a delicate chain around her neck. Her breath caught in her throat as she realized what it meant. "This necklace," Ethan began, his voice steady but filled with emotion, "it represents everything I love about you: your grace, your strength, your beauty. But it's also a symbol of something more—a symbol of my commitment to you." Samantha's eyes filled with tears as she looked up at him, her heart swelling with love. "Ethan..." Before she could say more, Ethan reached into his pocket and pulled out a small plush box. He opened it to reveal a simple yet elegant diamond ring that sparkled in the starlight. "Samantha, I've known for a long time that you're the one I want to spend the rest of my life with," Ethan said, his voice filled with sincerity. "You've brought so much joy and light into my life, and I can't imagine a future without you by my side. Will you marry me?" Tears spilled down Samantha's cheeks as she looked at the man she loved, the man who had become her best friend, her partner, and her home. "Yes," she whispered, her voice stifled with emotion. "Yes, I'll marry you." Ethan's face broke into a wide, joyful smile as he slipped the ring onto her finger. The fit was perfect, just like everything else between them. He pulled her into his arms, and they kissed under the stars, the world around them fading away as they lost themselves in each other. As they held each other close, the leaves continued to fall around them, a gentle reminder of the season of change they were in. But for Samantha and Ethan, this change was the start of something beautiful—an everlasting love that would carry them through all the seasons of their lives. They stood there for a long time, wrapped in each other's warmth, knowing that their journey together was only just beginning. The night air was cool, but Samantha felt nothing but the warmth of Ethan's love surrounding her. The future was bright, full of hope and promise, and she couldn't wait to spend every moment of it with him.

CHAPTER 9

A New Chapter Begins

The weeks following Ethan's proposal were a whirlwind of excitement and preparations. Samantha and Ethan dove into planning their wedding with enthusiasm, excitedly picking out venues, flowers, and decorations. The house they had recently moved into became a cozy hub of activity, filled with wedding magazines, sample swatches, and lists of to-dos. One Saturday morning, Samantha and Ethan decided to take a break from the planning chaos and enjoy a leisurely day together. They drove to a nearby park, where the last of the autumn leaves crunched underfoot, creating a picturesque scene perfect for a relaxing walk. As they walked hand in hand along the winding paths, Samantha couldn't help but marvel at how natural everything felt between them. Their conversations flowed effortlessly, and their shared laughter made her heart soar. Ethan suddenly stopped, pulling her to a halt beneath a grand oak tree with branches stretching high above them, still adorned with the vibrant colors of fall. "I've been thinking," he began, looking at her with a thoughtful expression. Samantha tilted her head, curious. "About what?" Ethan smiled, his eyes twinkling with a mix of mischief and affection. "About how we've been so focused on the wedding and the future that we haven't really taken a moment to just enjoy the present." Samantha nodded, her smile widening. "I know what you mean. It's easy to get caught up in all the details and forget to savor the little moments." Ethan reached into his jacket pocket and pulled out a small, leather-bound journal. "I thought it might be nice if we started keeping track of these little moments," he said, handing the journal to her. "We can write down our thoughts, our favorite memories, and anything else we want to remember." Samantha's eyes softened as she took the journal from him, touched by the gesture. "That's a wonderful idea," she said, her voice filled with warmth. "I'd love to." They spent the rest of the afternoon sitting under the oak tree, sharing their thoughts and dreams as they wrote in the journal. Ethan jotted down a few lines about their stroll and how much he cherished these simple moments with Samantha. Samantha wrote about her excitement for their future together and her gratitude for the love they shared. As the sun began to set, casting a golden glow over the park, they made their way back to the car, their hearts full and their spirits high. They drove home, talking about how much they were looking forward to the wedding day and the life they would build together. The next few weeks flew by in a flurry of final preparations and joyful anticipation. Samantha's bookstore was a hub of activity as she continued to work, managing to balance her professional life with the excitement of the wedding planning. Ethan was equally busy with work and finalizing the details for their big day. Finally, the day of the wedding arrived, and it was everything they had dreamed of. The ceremony took place in a charming garden venue adorned with fall foliage, the colors of autumn creating a breathtaking backdrop. Samantha, in a delicate lace wedding gown with a touch of vintage charm, looked radiant as she walked down the aisle on Ethan's arm. His eyes lit up with love and pride as he saw her, and he couldn't take his eyes off her throughout the ceremony. Their vows were heartfelt and sincere, each word reflecting the deep connection they shared. When they exchanged rings and were pronounced husband and wife, the joy in the air was palpable. Their first kiss as a married couple was tender and full of promise, a perfect start to their new life together. The reception was a joyous celebration, filled with laughter, dancing, and heartfelt toasts from friends and family. The evening was a perfect blend of elegance and warmth, with a festive atmosphere that matched the autumn season. Samantha and Ethan shared their first dance as a married couple, surrounded by the soft glow of fairy lights and the soothing strains of their favorite song. As the night wore on and the guests began to depart, Samantha and Ethan took a moment to step outside and enjoy the cool, crisp night air. The stars were shining brightly overhead, and the sound of leaves rustling in the gentle breeze created a serene backdrop. "This has been perfect," Samantha said, leaning into Ethan's embrace as they stood together beneath the stars. Ethan kissed the top of her head, his heart full of love and contentment. "It has." "And now the real adventure begins." Samantha looked up at him, her eyes shining with happiness. "I can't wait to see what the future holds for us." They stood there for a while, savoring the quiet and the closeness, knowing that this was just the beginning of their journey together. The love they shared was a beautiful, unbreakable bond that would carry them through all the seasons of their lives. As they eventually made their way back inside, hand in hand, Samantha felt a deep sense of peace and fulfillment. Their life together was a textile of shared moments, dreams, and endless love. And with Ethan by her side, she knew that no matter what challenges or joys lay ahead, they would face them together, with hearts full of love and whispers of "forever."

CHAPTER 10

The Honeymoon

After their magical wedding day, Samantha and Ethan set off for their honeymoon. They had chosen a cozy, secluded cabin in the mountains for a week of relaxation and romance. The cabin was nestled in a picturesque valley, surrounded by towering pines and serene lakes, offering them the perfect retreat from the hustle and bustle of everyday life. As they arrived at the cabin, the autumn landscape greeted them with a breathtaking display of colors. The air was crisp and fresh, and the leaves on the trees had transformed into a vibrant tapestry of red, orange, and gold. Samantha and Ethan unloaded their luggage, their excitement palpable as they took in the beauty of their surroundings. The cabin itself was charming and rustic, with a stone fireplace, wooden beams, and large windows that framed the stunning views of the mountains. The interior was warm and inviting, decorated with plush furnishings and cozy throws. They immediately felt at home. "We're going to love it here," Samantha said, her voice filled with anticipation as she looked around the cabin. Ethan grinned, wrapping his arms around her. "I know we will. It's perfect." Their days at the cabin were filled with simple pleasures. They spent their mornings sipping coffee on the porch, watching the mist lift from the valley below as the sun rose. They explored the nearby trails, taking leisurely hikes through the forest and along the shores of crystal-clear lakes. Each evening, they returned to the cabin, where they cooked meals together and enjoyed quiet nights by the fire. One evening, as the sun dipped below the horizon and the sky was painted in shades of pink and purple, Ethan set up a picnic on the porch. He had prepared a spread of Samantha's favorite foods—fresh bread, cheese, fruit, and a bottle of fine wine. Candles flickered softly in the breeze, casting a romantic glow over the scene. "This is wonderful," Samantha said, her eyes shining as she took in the picturesque setting. "I wanted to do something special for you," Ethan replied, pouring her a glass of wine. "You've made this week so magical." They spent the evening enjoying their meal, talking and laughing as the stars began to appear in the clear night sky. Afterward, they snuggled under a blanket, watching the moonlight dance on the surface of the lake. As the week went on, Samantha and Ethan continued to deepen their bond. They shared their hopes and dreams for the future, discussing everything from their plans for a family to their dreams of traveling the world. They also took time to simply enjoy each other's company, cherishing the quiet moments of intimacy and connection. One afternoon, while exploring a nearby trail, they stumbled upon a hidden waterfall. The sight was stunning, with water cascading down the rocks into a clear pool below. Ethan pulled Samantha close, his eyes reflecting the same sense of wonder and joy that she felt. "This place feels like a little piece of paradise," Samantha said, her voice filled with awe. "It does," Ethan agreed, his gaze fixed on her. "And I'm so grateful to be sharing it with you." As they stood there, the sound of the waterfall creating a soothing backdrop, Ethan took Samantha's hand and led her to the edge of the pool. He pulled her gently into his arms, and they shared a tender kiss, the water sparkling around them. The rest of their honeymoon passed in a blur of happiness and contentment. When it was time to leave, neither of them wanted to say goodbye to the cabin and the peaceful sanctuary it had provided. But as they packed up their belongings and prepared to head back to their new home, they knew that the memories they had created would stay with them forever. Returning to their daily lives, Samantha and Ethan felt more connected than ever. The cabin had given them the chance to pause and reflect on their relationship, reinforcing their commitment to each other and their shared dreams. Back at their house, they continued to build their life together, tackling new challenges and celebrating small victories. Their home was filled with the warmth of their love, and every day brought new opportunities for joy and growth. As the seasons changed and the leaves fell from the trees, Samantha and Ethan embraced the changes in their lives with the same love and enthusiasm that had marked their honeymoon. They knew that their journey together was just beginning, and with each passing day, they grew more excited about the future they would build side by side. Their love was a witness to the beauty of life's simple moments and the strength of their connection. And as they faced the adventures and challenges ahead, they did so with hearts full of hope and whispers of forever.

CHAPTER 11

Settling into New Rhythms

Returning from their honeymoon, Samantha and Ethan settled back into their daily lives with renewed energy and a deepened bond. Their new home, once a canvas of potential, now felt like a lived-in sanctuary filled with the warmth of their shared experiences. As autumn continued its gentle transformation into winter, Samantha busied herself with her photography and bookstore. She found a new rhythm in her work, infusing her projects with the inspiration she had gained from their time at the cabin. The bookstore became a cozy haven decorated with twinkling lights and seasonal touches, attracting customers seeking the comfort of a good book during the chilly months. Ethan, meanwhile, continued to immerse himself in his career, finding a satisfying balance between work and his new role as a husband. He often surprised Samantha with small, thoughtful gestures—flowers, handwritten notes, and impromptu date nights—each one a reminder of his love and appreciation. One crisp Saturday morning, Ethan approached Samantha with an idea. "How about a day off from our usual routines? I was thinking we could spend the day exploring some of the local winter markets. I've heard they're really charming this time of year." Samantha's eyes lit up with excitement. "That sounds perfect!" "I've been wanting to see more of what our town has to offer during the winter." They spent the day meandering through the bustling markets, enjoying the festive atmosphere and sampling delicious seasonal treats. They marveled at the array of handcrafted goods and artisanal products, and Ethan even bought Samantha a beautifully knitted scarf, its deep red hue perfect for the season. As the afternoon turned to evening, they stopped at a quaint café for hot chocolate and pastries. The café, with its rustic charm and crackling fireplace, provided a warm refuge from the cold outside. They sat by the window, watching the snow gently fall and the world outside transform into a winter fairyland. "This has been such a wonderful day," Samantha said, her voice filled with contentment. "I love how we're making new traditions together." Ethan smiled, reaching across the table to take her hand. "I do too." "Every day with you feels like a new adventure." Their evenings were often spent in the comfort of their home, where they would curl up together by the fireplace with a good book or simply enjoy each other's company. The holiday season brought a special magic to their home, with decorations and festive music adding to the cozy atmosphere. One evening, as they prepared for the New Year, Samantha surprised Ethan with a special gift. She had been working on a photo album filled with pictures from their honeymoon, their wedding, and their everyday life together. Each page was carefully crafted, capturing the essence of their journey as a couple. Ethan's eyes softened with emotion as he flipped through the album. "This is amazing, Samantha. Thank you." "I wanted to give you something to show how much you mean to me," Samantha said, her voice full of love. The New Year's Eve celebrations were intimate and joyful. They hosted a small gathering with close friends and family, sharing laughter and stories as they toasted to the year ahead. The evening ended with a quiet moment on the porch, where they watched the fireworks light up the night sky. As the first rays of the New Year dawned, Ethan and Samantha embraced, their hearts filled with hope and excitement for the future. They made their way back inside, where they spent the rest of the night talking about their dreams and aspirations for the coming year. With the arrival of the New Year, Samantha and Ethan continued to build their life together, embracing the changes and challenges that came their way. Their love grew stronger with each passing day, and they cherished the small moments of connection and joy that made their life together so special. The winter months passed in a blur of warmth and contentment, and as spring began to emerge, Samantha and Ethan looked forward to the new adventures that awaited them. They knew that their journey together was just beginning, and with hearts full of love and anticipation, they faced each day with appreciation and excitement.

CHAPTER 12

A New Outlook

Several months had passed since the New Year, and life for Samantha and Ethan had settled into a comforting rhythm. The winter snow had melted away, giving way to the fresh blossoms of spring. Their home was filled with the vibrant colors and scents of the season, and their days were marked by a sense of joy and anticipation. One sunny afternoon, as Samantha was arranging fresh flowers in the living room, she couldn't help but smile to herself. She had been planning a special surprise for Ethan, something she had been keeping a secret for weeks. As she looked around their home, she felt a thrill of excitement at the thought of sharing this news with him. Ethan had been working long hours at the office, and Samantha wanted to do something extra special to celebrate their upcoming weekend together. She decided to plan a surprise dinner at home, complete with Ethan's favorite dishes and a little extra something that would make the evening unforgettable. As the day drew to a close, Samantha put the finishing touches on the table setting, lit candles, and set out a delicious meal. When Ethan finally walked through the door, he was greeted by the warm glow of the candles and the enticing aroma of the food. "Wow, Samantha, this looks incredible," Ethan said, taking in the romantic setting. "What's the occasion?" Samantha's heart fluttered with excitement. "Just a little celebration," she said with a mysterious smile. "I wanted to do something special for us." They enjoyed a wonderful meal together, filled with laughter and heartfelt conversation. As they finished dessert, Samantha took a deep breath, feeling a mix of nerves and exhilaration. She knew this was the perfect moment to share her news. "Ethan," she began, reaching into her purse and pulling out a small, neatly wrapped box, "there's something I've been meaning to give you." Ethan looked at the box with inquisitiveness as he took it from her. "What's this?" Samantha nodded, her eyes shining with anticipation. "Open it and see." Ethan carefully unwrapped the box, revealing a tiny pair of baby booties nestled inside. He looked up at Samantha, confusion and then realization dawning in his eyes. "Are these...?" Samantha's eyes filled with tears of joy as she nodded. "Yes, Ethan. We're going to have a baby." Ethan's expression transformed from surprise to pure, overwhelming happiness. He stood up and crossed the room, pulling Samantha into a tight embrace. "Are you serious? This is incredible!" Samantha laughed, her tears of joy mixing with his. "Yes, I'm serious." "I've been to the doctor, and everything is going well?" "I wanted to wait until now to tell you, so we could celebrate together." Ethan pulled back slightly, holding Samantha's face in his hands. "I can't believe it. This is the best news ever. I'm so excited to be a dad." The evening turned into a celebration of their new journey as they talked about their hopes and dreams for their baby. They spent hours discussing names, decorating ideas for the nursery, and their plans for the future. The love and excitement they felt were palpable, filling their home with a new kind of warmth. A few weeks later, they had their first ultrasound appointment.

As they entered the dimly lit room, Ethan squeezed Samantha's hand for support. The technician smiled warmly as she prepared the ultrasound equipment. "Are you ready to see your baby?" the technician asked, glancing at them. Samantha and Ethan nodded eagerly, their hearts racing with anticipation. As the technician moved the wand across Samantha's belly, the image on the screen came into focus. Ethan's eyes widened with awe as he saw the tiny, fluttering figure of their baby. "That's our little one," he said, his voice filled with wonder. The technician pointed out the baby's features and confirmed that everything looked healthy. Then, with a gentle smile, she added, "It looks like you're having a little girl." Samantha and Ethan exchanged a look of pure joy. The news of their baby girl made everything feel even more real and special. They talked excitedly about names, imagining the future with their daughter and the joy she would bring to their lives. As they left the appointment, Samantha and Ethan felt a renewed sense of excitement and connection. Their future was unfolding in beautiful and unexpected ways, and they were ready to embrace every moment of it. Back at home, they began preparing for their baby girl's arrival, transforming a spare room into a nursery and filling it with love and anticipation. The once-quiet house now buzzed with the promise of new beginnings, and Samantha and Ethan were ready to embark on this new chapter of their lives together.

Preparing for Katelyn

As spring gave way to summer, Samantha and Ethan's home buzzed with preparations for the arrival of their baby girl, Katelyn. The nursery took shape, evolving into a haven of soft pastels and cozy comforts. They chose a gentle palette of blush pinks and serene greens, with delicate floral patterns and plush, inviting furnishings. Samantha spent her afternoons arranging the nursery, carefully hanging up tiny clothes, and organizing the shelves. Ethan, equally excited, assembled furniture and installed the finishing touches, his hands working with a newfound tenderness. They enjoyed these moments together, imagining their life with Katelyn and the joy she would bring. One evening, as they sat together on the porch enjoying a warm summer breeze, Ethan turned to Samantha with a thoughtful expression. "I was thinking about how much we've been preparing for Katelyn." "Maybe we should take a little break and do something fun together before she arrives." Samantha smiled, her eyes sparkling with excitement. "That sounds like a great idea. What did you have in mind?" Ethan grinned. "How about a weekend getaway to the beach? We could relax and enjoy some quiet time before everything gets even busier." Samantha's face lit up. "That sounds perfect!" "I've been wanting to spend some time by the ocean." They planned a short trip to a charming coastal town, where they could unwind and soak up the sun before Katelyn's arrival. The beach house they rented was cozy and inviting, with a view of the ocean and easy access to the sandy shores. Their days were filled with leisurely walks along the beach, collecting seashells, and savoring fresh seafood at local restaurants. They enjoyed lazy afternoons lounging on the sand, with Ethan often playfully teasing Samantha as they splashed in the waves. One evening, as the sun set over the horizon and painted the sky in shades of orange and pink, they sat together on the beach, wrapped in a blanket. The sound of the waves crashing against the shore provided a soothing soundtrack to their quiet moment. "I'm so glad we took this trip," Samantha said, leaning against Ethan. "It's been wonderful to relax and enjoy each other's company." Ethan kissed the top of her head, his heart full of contentment. "Me too. It's been a perfect escape before our new adventure begins." They spent the remainder of the trip enjoying each other's company and the peaceful surroundings. As they drove back home, their hearts were full of anticipation for the arrival of their daughter and the life they would soon share as a family. Back at home, the final preparations for Katelyn's arrival were underway. Samantha and Ethan worked together to finish the nursery, and soon it was ready—complete with a crib adorned with soft bedding, a rocking chair for late-night feedings, and a collection of cherished toys. The weeks flew by, and soon, Samantha's due date approached. The anticipation was palpable, and every day brought them one step closer to meeting their baby girl. Friends and family showered them with love and support, offering advice and sharing in their excitement. One warm summer afternoon, Samantha and

Ethan took a break from their preparations to visit a local park. They strolled hand in hand, talking about their hopes and dreams for Katelyn and the future. As they walked, Ethan gently placed his hand on Samantha's belly, feeling the gentle movements of their daughter. "I can't wait to hold her," Ethan said softly. "I already love her so much." Samantha smiled, her eyes misty with emotion. "I know. It's hard to believe that we'll be meeting her soon." Their conversations were filled with plans for their new life as parents, and they cherished these moments of connection and anticipation. They were ready for the changes that lay ahead, excited to welcome Katelyn into their lives and begin this new chapter of their journey together. As the days passed and Samantha's due date approached, they found themselves counting down the moments until they could finally hold their baby girl. Their home was filled with the promise of new beginnings, and they eagerly awaited the arrival of Katelyn, ready to embrace the joys and challenges of parenthood.

The Arrival of Katelyn

The days leading up to Samantha's due date were filled with a blend of excitement and nervous anticipation. Their home was a picture of preparedness, with the nursery fully set up and everything in place for their baby's arrival. Samantha and Ethan had attended all their prenatal appointments and had carefully reviewed their birth plan, eager and ready for the big moment. On the morning of Samantha's due date, the sky was clear, and a gentle breeze rustled the leaves outside. Samantha woke up feeling a mix of excitement and nervousness, knowing that today could be the day they would meet their daughter. Ethan, equally anxious and thrilled, stayed close by, supporting Samantha through every moment. As the day went on, Samantha began to feel the early signs of labor. She and Ethan made their way to the hospital, their hearts racing with anticipation. The drive was filled with a quiet intensity, punctuated by soft, reassuring words from Ethan and Samantha's focused breathing. At the hospital, the medical team prepared for their arrival, ensuring that everything was in place for the delivery. Samantha was admitted and settled into a labor room, where she was surrounded by calming colors and the comforting presence of Ethan. They worked together to manage the contractions, and Ethan stayed by Samantha's side, holding her hand and offering words of encouragement. Hours passed, and the labor progressed. Samantha's strength and determination were evident, and Ethan admired her resilience through each contraction. The support of the medical team and Ethan's presence made the experience more manageable, even as the anticipation grew. Finally, after a long and intense labor, the moment arrived. With a final push, the room was filled with the sound of a baby's first cry. Samantha and Ethan looked at each other, their eyes filled with tears of joy and relief. The nurse carefully placed their newborn daughter in Samantha's arms, and Ethan leaned in to see her. "She's beautiful," he whispered, his voice choked with emotion. Their baby girl was named Katelyn Grace Carter. She weighed 7 pounds, 4 ounces, and measured 19 inches long. Her tiny fingers and toes, and the soft tuft of dark hair on her head, were perfect in every way. Samantha looked down at Katelyn, feeling an overwhelming sense of love and wonder. "Welcome to the world, Katelyn," she said softly, her voice trembling with emotion. Ethan gently touched Katelyn's cheek, his heart swelling with pride and affection. "You're perfect, Katelyn. We've been waiting for you." The next few hours were filled with family and friends visiting, all eager to meet the newest addition to their lives. Samantha and Ethan basked in the joy of introducing Katelyn to her loved ones, who showered her with affection and warm wishes. As they settled into the rhythm of their new life as parents, Samantha and Ethan found a deep sense of fulfillment and happiness. They cherished the quiet moments spent with Katelyn, marveling at her tiny features and the soft sounds of her breathing. The first few weeks with Katelyn were filled with both challenges and immense joy. Samantha and Ethan adjusted to the demands of parenthood, finding their own rhythm and learning the nuances of caring for their daughter. They took turns tending to Katelyn's needs, sharing in the responsibilities and the joy of their new role. Their home was now filled with the sounds of a baby's laughter and the comforting routines of feeding, changing, and soothing. The nursery, once a room awaiting its occupant, had become a vibrant space of love and care, with Katelyn's every need met and her arrival celebrated. As the days turned into weeks, Samantha and Ethan embraced their new life with Katelyn, savoring each precious moment and looking forward to the many adventures ahead. Their hearts were full, and their family was complete with the arrival of their beautiful baby girl.

CHAPTER 15

Uncovering The History

The crisp autumn breeze swept through the town of Maplewood, carrying with it the scent of pine and damp earth. The leaves had begun their descent from the trees, painting the streets in shades of gold, red, and orange. Samantha strolled through the quiet streets, her thoughts as scattered as the leaves around her. It had been a few months since the mysterious notes and flowers from Ethan first appeared, leading to their blossoming romance. Their relationship had deepened, yet something about it lingered in the back of Samantha's mind—a feeling that Ethan was holding something back. As she reached her bookstore, the sun dipped below the horizon, casting long shadows across the sidewalk. Samantha turned the key in the lock and pushed open the door, the familiar scent of old paper and freshly brewed coffee welcoming her. The bookstore had become her sanctuary, a place where she could lose herself in stories and escape the complexities of her own life. But today, as she walked through the rows of books, she couldn't shake the feeling that something was off. Her eyes fell on the corner table where Ethan often sat waiting for her. Today, however, the table was empty, save for an individual white envelope. Her heart skipped a beat as she approached the table, picking up the envelope. Her name was written in Ethan's elegant handwriting. She hesitated for a moment before tearing it open, revealing a single piece of paper inside. "Meet me at the old lighthouse tonight. I have something important to tell you." Samantha's breath caught in her throat. The old lighthouse on the outskirts of town had long been abandoned, standing as a lonely sentinel against the rugged cliffs. It was a place of quiet solitude, where the sea met the sky in endless, crashing waves. "Why there?" she wondered. And what was so important that it couldn't wait until tomorrow? Without a second thought, Samantha grabbed her coat and keys, her mind racing with possibilities. She knew Ethan well enough to trust him, but the mystery of his note filled her with a sense of urgency she couldn't ignore.

CHAPTER 16

Silhouette of the Past

The drive to the lighthouse was a solitary one, the winding road lined with towering trees that seemed to close in around her as the darkness deepened. Samantha's mind replayed the events of the past few months, searching for any clue she might have missed—anything that could explain why Ethan had chosen such an isolated place for their meeting. When she finally reached the lighthouse, the structure loomed against the dark sky, its weathered stones bathed in the pale light of the moon. The sound of the waves crashing against the rocks below was louder here, a constant roar that drowned out the silence of the night. Samantha stepped out of her car, the cold sea air biting at her skin. She wrapped her coat tighter around her and made her way toward the lighthouse. As she approached, she saw Ethan standing near the entrance, his back to her as he stared out at the ocean. "Ethan," she called out, her voice carried away by the wind. He turned to face her, his expression unreadable. For a moment, they stood in silence, the distance between them feeling greater than it ever had before. "I'm glad you came," Ethan finally said, his voice low and strained. "Of course I came,"

Samantha replied, trying to keep the anxiety out of her voice. "What's going on? Why did you ask me to meet you here?" Ethan took a deep breath, his gaze shifting to the lighthouse behind him. "There's something I need to tell you, Samantha." "Something I should have told you a long time ago." The tension in his voice was palpable, and Samantha's heart pounded in her chest. "What is it? You're scaring me." Ethan took a step closer, reaching for her hand. "It's about my past. There's something I've been keeping from you—something that I've been afraid to share because I didn't want to lose you." Samantha's mind raced. Was it another woman? A dark secret he had been hiding? The possibilities seemed endless, and each one was worse than the last. Ethan's grip on her hand tightened as he continued. "Before I met you, I was involved in something... something dangerous. It wasn't just my work; it was personal. I got caught up with the wrong people, and it's something I've been trying to put behind me ever since." Samantha felt a chill run down her spine, but she forced herself to listen and understand. "What do you mean?" "What kind of people?" Ethan hesitated, his jaw clenched as if he were struggling to find the right words. "Let's go inside. There's something I need to show you. It's the only way you'll understand." Without waiting for her response, he turned and led her into the lighthouse. The door creaked open, revealing the dusty interior, lit only by the moonlight filtering through the narrow windows. Ethan guided her up the spiral staircase, their footsteps echoing in the empty space.At the top, they entered a small room with a single table in the center. On the table was a leather-bound notebook, worn and weathered with age. Ethan picked it up and handed it to her. "This belonged to my father," Ethan explained. "He was a journalist, always chasing the next big story. But his last story... it got him killed." Samantha's hands trembled as she opened the notebook. The pages were filled with handwritten notes, articles, and photographs, all detailing an investigation into a criminal syndicate that operated under the radar, evading the law for years. "He was onto something big," Ethan continued. "But before he could expose them, he disappeared." "The police never found his body, but I know those people were responsible." "I've been trying to figure out who they are and what they're after ever since." Samantha stared at the notebook, the pieces of the puzzle slowly falling into place. "So that's why you've been so secretive? You've been investigating this on your own?" Ethan nodded, his expression grave. "I didn't want to drag you into this, Samantha." But I realized I can't keep it from you anymore. I'm getting close to finding out the truth, and that means I'm putting myself—and you—in danger. Samantha's heart ached with the weight of his words. She had always known there was more to Ethan than met the eye, but this was beyond anything she had imagined. Yet, despite the fear gnawing at her, she felt a surge of determination. "We'll figure this out together," she said firmly. "I'm not going to let you face this alone." Ethan's eyes softened, and he pulled her into a tight embrace. "I don't deserve you, Samantha. But I promise I'll do everything I can to keep you safe." As they stood together in the old lighthouse, surrounded by the shadows of the past, Samantha knew their journey was far from over. The truth about Ethan's father, the criminal syndicate, and the dangers that lay ahead would test their love and their resolve. But no matter what came next, she was ready to face it, as long as they faced it together.

CHAPTER 17

In the Shadows

n the days that followed, Samantha and Ethan delved deeper into his father's investigation. The notebook provided clues, but it was clear that Ethan's father had been onto something far more sinister than they initially thought. The syndicate wasn't just a group of criminals; they were deeply embedded in the town of Maplewood, with ties to influential figures and businesses. As they uncovered more, Samantha began to notice strange occurrences around the bookstore. People she didn't recognize would linger outside, watching her with a little too much interest. The phone would ring, and no one would be on the other end. Even the once-familiar faces in town seemed to hold secrets behind their polite smiles. One evening, as Samantha was closing up the bookstore, she received a package. It was a plain brown box with no return address. Her name was scrawled on the top in an unfamiliar hand. With a sense of unease, she brought the package inside and opened it. Inside, she found a small silver locket and a note that read: "Trust no one. They're closer than you think." Samantha's blood ran cold. She turned the locket over in her hand, finding an engraving on the back that matched the symbol she had seen in Ethan's father's notebook. She knew then that they were being watched. The syndicate was aware of their investigation, and they were sending a message—a warning. But Samantha refused to back down. If anything, the threat only strengthened her resolve. She and Ethan would continue their search for the truth, no matter the cost.

Untangling the Web

The deeper they dug, the more they realized just how far the syndicate's reach extended. They uncovered connections between the town's most respected citizens and the shadowy organization, revealing a network of corruption and deceit that spanned decades. But as they got closer to uncovering the syndicate's leaders, the danger increased. One night, Ethan's car was tampered with, and he barely escaped a serious accident. Another time, Samantha returned to her bookstore to find it ransacked, though nothing appeared to be stolen. The final straw came when she received an anonymous tip directing her to an abandoned warehouse on the outskirts of town. There, she found documents that confirmed their worst fears: the syndicate was planning something big, something that could bring the entire town to its knees.

Untangling the Web (Continued)

CHAPTER 18

: But before they could leave, they were ambushed. A group of men dressed in dark clothing, their faces obscured by shadows, surrounded them. Ethan pushed Samantha behind him, his eyes scanning the room for a way out. "Run, Samantha!" he shouted, his voice filled with urgency. Samantha hesitated for a split second, fear gripping her, but then she turned and ran, her heart pounding in her chest. She heard the sound of a struggle behind her, but she didn't dare look back. The narrow hallways of the warehouse twisted and turned, and she could hear footsteps closing in behind her. She stumbled through a side door, emerging into the cold night air. The sky was a dark canvas, with only a sliver of moonlight guiding her path. She could barely see in the darkness, but she knew she had to keep moving. Suddenly, strong arms grabbed her from behind, pulling her back into the shadows. She fought against her captor, but he was too strong. As she struggled, she heard a familiar voice whisper in her ear. "Samantha, it's me!" It was Ethan. He had somehow managed to escape and find her. Relief flooded through her as he pulled her into a hidden alcove, where they crouched together, trying to catch their breath. "They were waiting for us," Ethan said, his voice low and tense. "We need to get out of here. They'll have the whole place locked down soon." Samantha nodded, her mind racing. "But where do we go?" "They know we're onto them." "We're not safe anywhere in Maplewood." Ethan hesitated, then said, "There's one place they won't expect us to go: the old Carter estate, on the outskirts of town. It's been abandoned for years, but it's still in my family's name. We can hide there until we figure out our next move." Samantha wasn't thrilled about the idea of hiding out in an abandoned mansion, but they didn't have many options. She trusted Ethan, and if he thought it was their best chance, she would follow him. They made their way through the dark, using the shadows to their advantage. The town was eerily quiet as they reached the estate, a grand but decaying building surrounded by overgrown gardens. It had once been a symbol of wealth and power, but now it stood as a ghostly reminder of a bygone era. Ethan led Samantha inside, and they found a dusty room on the second floor where they could rest. As they sat in the darkness, surrounded by the echoes of the past, Samantha felt the weight of everything they had uncovered pressing down on her. "We need to end this," she whispered, her voice trembling. "We need to expose them." Ethan nodded, his expression determined. "We will." "But we have to be smart about it." "We need evidence—something concrete that we can take to the authorities." As they sat together, planning their next steps, Samantha couldn't shake the feeling that they were racing against time. The syndicate was closing in, and they wouldn't stop until Ethan and Samantha were silenced for good. But Samantha was done running. She was ready to fight back, no matter the cost.

CHAPTER 19

The Final Disruption

The next few days were a blur of tension and fear as Samantha and Ethan prepared to make their move. They knew that the syndicate would stop at nothing to protect their secrets, and the only way to bring them down was to gather irrefutable evidence and expose them to the world. Ethan spent hours going through the documents they had found at the warehouse, piecing together the syndicate's operations and their connections to powerful figures in Maplewood. It was a dangerous game, but every piece of the puzzle brought them one step closer to the truth. Meanwhile, Samantha reached out to an old friend, a journalist she trusted, and arranged a secret meeting. They needed someone with the resources and reach to help them take down the syndicate, and her friend, Mia, was the perfect ally. When Mia arrived at the estate, Samantha and Ethan laid everything out for her—the documents, the notes, the photographs, and the names of those involved. Mia was shocked by what she saw, but she was also determined to help. "This is huge," Mia said, her voice trembling with excitement. "We can't let them get away with this. But we have to be careful. If they catch wind of what we're doing, they'll come after us hard." Ethan nodded. "That's why we're going to hit them fast and hard. We've already risked too much to back down now." Mia agreed to take the evidence and start working on a series of articles that would expose the syndicate's crimes. But first, they needed a way to ensure their safety. Mia suggested they go public with a teaser—just enough to let the syndicate know that their secrets were no longer safe. The plan was set in motion, and the first article was published, hinting at the corruption and criminal activities that had been festering in Maplewood for years. It sent shockwaves through the town, and the syndicate's leaders were thrown into a frenzy. Samantha and Ethan knew it was only a matter of time before the syndicate made their move, so they prepared for the inevitable confrontation. They set traps around the estate and enlisted the help of a few trusted friends to guard the perimeter. As night fell, the tension in the air was palpable. The wind howled through the trees, and the old mansion creaked under the pressure of the coming storm. Samantha and Ethan stood together in the dusty room, their hearts racing as they awaited the syndicate's arrival. "We're going to get through this," Ethan said, his voice steady despite the fear in his eyes. Samantha nodded, squeezing his hand. "We have to. For your father, for the town... and for us." The sound of footsteps outside shattered the silence, and they knew the time had come. The final showdown was about to begin, and there was no turning back.

CHAPTER 20

The Restlessness

The syndicate's enforcers arrived under the cover of darkness, their footsteps heavy and deliberate as they approached the estate. Ethan and Samantha watched from the second-floor window, their hearts pounding in their chests. "They're here," Ethan whispered, his hand tightening around the handle of the gun he had taken from his father's old collection. Samantha swallowed hard, her eyes locked on the approaching figures. There was no mistaking their intent—they were here to silence them once and for all. As the enforcers reached the front door, the traps Ethan had set sprang into action. Explosive charges detonated, sending the intruders scrambling for cover. But the enforcers were relentless, quickly recovering and storming the entrance. Ethan and Samantha retreated to their makeshift command center in the old study, where they had set up a network of cameras and traps throughout the mansion. They watched the monitors as the enforcers moved through the house, their movements precise and coordinated. "They're not going to stop," Samantha said, her voice trembling with fear. Ethan shook his head. "No, they won't. But we're not going to let them win."

They lured the enforcers into the mansion's various traps, using their knowledge of the estate's layout to their advantage. One by one, the intruders were taken out, but the odds were still stacked against them. As the final wave of enforcers reached the second floor, Ethan and Samantha knew they had to make their last stand. They barricaded themselves in the study, knowing that it would only buy them a few precious minutes. "Samantha," Ethan said, his voice filled with emotion, "I need you to know that no matter what happens, I love you. I always have, and I always will." Tears welled up in Samantha's eyes as she nodded. "I love you too, Ethan. We'll get through this together." The door to the study burst open, and the final confrontation began. Ethan and Samantha fought with everything they had, using the traps and their wits to hold off the enforcers. The struggle was intense, but in the end, they managed to overpower their attackers. As the last enforcer fell, silence filled the room. Ethan and Samantha stood there, breathing heavily, their bodies bruised and battered but alive. They had survived the night, but the war was far from over.

CHAPTER 21

Exposing the Truth

With the immediate threat neutralized, Ethan and Samantha knew they had to act quickly to expose the syndicate before it could regroup. Mia had already published the first article, but now they needed to deliver the final blow. They gathered all the evidence they had collected and worked with Mia to release a series of explosive exposés that laid bare the syndicate's operations, its leaders, and their crimes. The articles sent shockwaves through Maplewood and beyond, leading to arrests and investigations at the highest levels. The town that had once been under the syndicate's shadow was finally waking up to the truth, and the people responsible for so much pain and suffering were being brought to justice. Samantha and Ethan, though exhausted and still reeling from their ordeal, found solace in knowing that their fight had made a difference. They had risked everything, but in the end, they had prevailed.

Epilogue

A NEW SUNRISE

Months had passed since the night of the final showdown, and Maplewood was slowly beginning to heal. The town had changed, and so had Samantha and Ethan. They stood together on the cliff near the old lighthouse, the place where it had all begun. The sun was rising over the horizon, casting a warm, golden glow across the landscape. The waves crashed against the rocks below, a soothing rhythm that echoed the calm now settling over their lives. Samantha leaned into Ethan's side, her head resting on his shoulder. They had been through so much, but they had emerged stronger, not just as individuals but as a couple. The trials they had faced had forged an unbreakable bond between them. "Do you ever think about what might have happened if we hadn't uncovered the truth?" Samantha asked softly, her eyes fixed on the horizon. Ethan nodded, his gaze following hers. "All the time." "But I don't regret anything." "We did what we had to do, and we made a difference. That's what matters." Samantha smiled, feeling a sense of peace she hadn't known in months. "You're right. And now, we can finally move on. Together." Ethan turned to face her, his eyes filled with love and determination. "Together," he echoed, his voice firm. "Whatever comes next, we'll face it side by side." Samantha reached up and cupped his face in her hands, pulling him down for a slow, lingering kiss. It was a kiss that spoke of all the love they had for each other, of the battles they had fought and won, and of the future they were ready to embrace. When they finally pulled apart, Samantha looked into Ethan's eyes and saw the same hope and promise reflected back at her. They had endured so much darkness, but now, the light of a new dawn was shining on them. They stayed there for a while longer, watching as the sun climbed higher in the sky, symbolizing the new beginning they were about to embark on. The town of Maplewood would always be a part of their story, but it no longer held the power to define them. Together, they turned away from the cliff, hand in hand, ready to face whatever the future might bring. They had found their way back to each other, and no matter what challenges lay ahead, they knew they could overcome anything—as long as they were together. And so, with their hearts full of hope and love, Samantha and Ethan walked into the light of a new day, leaving the shadows of the past behind them.

The End